Fay Cow
and the
Missing Milk

Also by Peter Hunt

Fay Cow and the Missing Milk

Peter Hunt

Illustrated by
Duncan Smith

Julia MacRae Books
A division of Walker Books

For Sarah

Text © 1989 Peter Hunt
Illustrations © 1989 Duncan Smith
All rights reserved
First published in Great Britain 1989 by
Julia MacRae Books
A division of Walker Books
87 Vauxhall Walk
London, SE11 5HJ

British Library Cataloguing in Publication Data
Hunt, Peter, 1945–
Fay cow and the missing milk
I. Title
823'.914 [J]

ISBN 0-86203-384-5

Typeset by Graphicraft Typesetters Ltd, Hong Kong
Printed and bound in Great Britain by
BPCC Hazell Books Ltd
Member of BPCC Ltd
Aylesbury, Bucks, England

Chapter 1

There was a large chocolate pudding sitting in the field.

It was early morning, and early July, and Jill and Alice were standing on the second bar of the five-bar gate. There was a thin layer of mist, and it seemed as though the chocolate pudding was sitting in a sea of thin cream.

Alice's mother was walking across the field, carrying two empty, shining buckets.

Jill said, "Well, I'm sorry I didn't believe you. What's she called?"

"Fay Cow," said Alice. "She's got horns on the front, but I don't think she knows what to do with them."

"You confused me when you said she was a House Cow," Jill said. "I thought she lived in a house."

Alice's mother was leaving a pattern of dark footprints on the pale grass.

"She doesn't live in a house," Alice said. "She gives milk *to* a house. Well, two houses, actually. Ours and Simon's." Fay Cow belonged to Alice's mother and Simon's mother, and they shared the food they put in one end, and the milk that came out of the other end, and took turns to do the milking. People usually said that the best idea would be to own the back half, but Jill hadn't said it yet. She had only just arrived in the village, but she wasn't too bad so far.

This morning it was Alice's mother's turn to milk. "Fay Cow lives here." Alice pointed over her shoulder to the muddy yard, with

its broken-down barn with chickens scuffing in and out of the door, and the old plum-trees hanging over the wall.

Fay Cow seemed to be very comfortable on the grass, and chewed, her jaw going sideways left and then sideways right.

"She must be squashing the milk," Jill said.

Alice said, "Come on," and they opened the gate and sploshed through the mud to Fay Cow's barn. Inside there were low beams and loops of cobwebs. Jill stood in the doorway, thinking that where there were huge cobwebs there might be huge spiders.

In one corner was a large metal bin. Alice leaned down into it so that only her legs were showing, and came out with a handful of dusty round pellets.

"These are cow nuts," she said. "Fay Cow loves them." And, sure enough, when Alice went and held them in front of Fay Cow's nose, she heaved herself up. Now she looked like a brown barrel on four sticks. Alice backed away into the barn followed by Fay Cow and Alice's mother and the buckets. Jill watched from the doorway.

Alice's mother wiped down Fay Cow's udders with a sponge, and then she sat down with her cheek against Fay Cow's side, and began to pull at the teats. Fay Cow ignored her, and began to eat hay out of her rack.

Milk squirted into the bottom of the bucket with a hard sound hitting the metal, and then became a rhythm of small drilling noises.

By the time the buckets were full, and Fay Cow had been pushed out

into the field again, the sun was
warm, and the mist had cleared
away. Alice and Jill shut the gate
and put the rusty chain over the
gatepost. A black cat watched
them. They walked across Fay
Cow's field and into the steep lane,
where the hedges lifted over their
heads, all green with the sunshine.

At the bottom of the valley was a stream where the ducks sat on the bank. Some of them put their heads away, and two of them toppled over into the water and floated. There were two cottages on the far side of the stream. The first was Simon's,

with a plank bridge leading to it.
All the curtains in the cottage
windows were drawn. Alice's
mother put the buckets into the
stream, under the bridge.

"We leave it there to cool," Alice
said. "The stream's too shallow in
our garden."

Jill looked at the buckets. "It
doesn't look very safe," she said.

"Of course it's safe," Alice said,
although there had been one day
when there was a rainstorm and all
the water had swept the buckets
and all the milk away. But that
wasn't what Jill meant. She meant
that in town, somebody would have
stolen it.

"Come and have breakfast,"
Alice said, "and then Mummy's
going to make some cheese." Her
mother looked rather worried.
"What's the matter?" Alice said.

"It's just funny," Alice's mother
said. "Fay Cow gives much more
milk in the mornings than she does
in the evenings. I wonder what's
wrong?"

"You mean some of the milk's
missing?" Alice said.

"Looks like it."

"I knew it wasn't safe," Jill said.

Chapter 2

After breakfast, which was fresh bread and fresh Fay Cow milk and fresh butter made out of Fay Cow milk, Alice's mother started to make some cheese.

Outside the front door was a small patch of gravel path and grass, with Alice's slide on it, before you came to the stream. Jill helped Alice and her mother to pull a plastic dustbin and what looked like an old washing machine out of the kitchen. They put the dustbin into the washing machine. Then they brought buckets of milk from the kitchen, and poured them into the dustbin, and buckets of water from the stream which they poured into the washing machine around the dustbin.

"Is this how you make cheese?" Jill said.

"Well, we don't shake Fay Cow up and down," Alice said. "Don't look so worried. That's a boiler that the dustbin's in. It warms up the milk, and then you add some secret stuff and it turns into sort of blancmange. That's all we use the dustbin for."

They went into the low kitchen. "We'll make some butter while

we're waiting."

Every morning, the Faymilk was
poured into big shallow plastic
boxes, and after a while the cream
came to the top. Alice's mother
scraped it off with a big spoon, and

collected it in another big plastic
box. This box was sitting on the
wooden worktop. Alice found the
electric mixer (the one you could
hold in your hands), and she held it
into the cream, and pressed the
button. It zizzed, and the cream
curled up around it in a moving
wave shape.

"I thought you needed a churn or something," Jill said.

"That's how they used to do it," Alice said. "All you need now is a zizzer."

"Can I have a go?" Jill said.

"As long as you keep it under the surface," Alice said. "If you let it come up, it sprays all over the walls and we get sent out."

So they took turns, and after about five minutes the buzz of the mixer went deeper, and the cream hardened and stopped being cream.

"Now we have to wash it," Alice said. "I'll get the Scotch Hands."

By this time, Jill had learned not to ask about things like that, and the Scotch Hands turned out to be little wooden paddles, like table-tennis bats.

They put the yellow lumps of solid cream into a bowl of water, and then rolled and squashed them between the paddles. Drops of water came out.

"Butter," said Alice. "Come and see the cheese."

They went out of the kitchen and through a low door, and down steep stone steps into the cellar. Alice reached around in the half-light and found a switch. A single bulb came on.

"This always fills up with water in the winter," Alice said.

Jill decided that there wasn't any
need to make up stories when you
lived in the country, what with cows
and cellars, and cheeses.

In one corner of the stone cellar
was a curious-looking object like a
huge corkscrew. Underneath it was
something wrapped in what looked
like a nappy.

"See," Alice said. "That's a

cheese being pressed. You come
down and turn the handle every
day, and the cheese gets cheesier."
And over their heads, hanging from
the rafters, were rope nets of
cheeses, yellow, and orange.

They were playing on the slide
(with mouthfuls of cheese from the
fridge) when Simon's mother came
into the garden to get the empty
buckets. It was her turn to milk that
evening and the next morning.
Simon came with her.

"Oh, no," Alice said. "Just ignore
him." But it was a bit difficult. The
mothers went into the kitchen to
talk about Fay Cow and the milk
mystery. Simon's mother hadn't

noticed that any milk *was* missing.

Jill and Alice and Simon looked at each other. Then they started to slide on the slide, taking turns, until Simon began to climb back up the slide rather than going up the

steps. Then he wouldn't get off at all, and when Alice tried to get past him, he pushed her so hard that she skidded off the slide and off the grass onto the gravel, and scraped the skin off her right elbow. She wasn't crying, but her face had gone very pale and quiet.

Simon's mother came out of the house, and said, "Say sorry, Simon," without looking at them. She picked up the empty buckets, and went back towards her house. "High spirits," she said, over her shoulder. Simon went with her, through the gap in the hedge.

Jill picked up a handful of gravel to throw, and then let it dribble

onto the ground.

"High spirits," she said. "He's like that at school. I hate him."

Alice had started to cry, rather quietly, because you didn't let someone like Simon see that he could make you. She dipped her handkerchief into the stream, and held it cool on her arm.

After a while, her mother came out and they lifted the dustbin out of the boiler, and tilted it over the stream. A thin liquid ran out and clouded the water, and then it ran away. Alice and Jill looked inside. There was a large white lump of something, wobbling. Alice's mother went back into the kitchen, and

came out with a carving knife. Jill
stepped back, nearly into the
stream. The carving knife was for
stabbing the white stuff with.
Curiouser and curiouser.

"You've got to cheddar it," Alice
said. "That means you cut it up,
and stack it, and drain it, then you
do it again, and then you do it lots
more times and it turns into
cheese."

"You're making Cheddar cheese, then," Jill said.

"No," said Alice. "I think we're making Cheshire. But you have to cheddar it anyway." Jill opened her mouth, then closed it again. Alice said: "Then you wrap the curd up in muslin – well, Mummy uses my old nappies – washed, of course – and then you press it."

"I want a word with you two," Alice's mother said. She had

finished turning the pieces of white curd. She wiped her hands on her long apron. "I've just been hearing about Simon. His mummy's very upset because she says you're being nasty to him at school."

"We're not," Alice said. "We just don't talk to him much. At all."

"He's very nasty to everybody," Jill said.

"And that's typical," Alice said. "Sneaking to his mum."

"You'd be nasty if nobody talked to you," Alice's mother said.

"But that's why we don't," Alice said. "I mean, he was nasty to us before we started stopping talking to him."

"Listen," Alice's mother said. "I said I'd make you promise to be nice to him from now on."

"Why?" said Alice.

"Because his daddy's away a lot," Alice's mother said.

"Why?" said Alice.

"Because they're not very friendly at the moment," Alice's mother said. "That means that Simon and his mummy haven't got much money, and so his mummy has to work late all the time, and that makes her tired."

"So is that any reason for pushing?" Alice said. "He pushed Jill off the wall after church last Sunday."

"It means," Alice's mother said, "that she's tired and he's tired, and it's very sad. Just think what you'd feel like if your daddy went away."

Alice looked very dubious. She said: "OK, we'll try. But can we

have a deal?" She looked at Jill. "We always have deals in our family." Jill said nothing.

"That depends," Alice's mother said.

"Can we have a picnic in Fay Cow's field tomorrow morning? Just me and Jill?"

"Why? If you don't mind my asking?"

"We're going to solve the mystery of the milk," Alice said. "We think somebody must be milking Fay Cow before you do, if there's less milk."

"Perhaps it's foxes," Jill said. Alice looked at her. "Well," Jill said, "my mum says she read a book where it said foxes can suck the milk out of cows when they get hungry. The foxes, that is."

Alice still looked at her.

"I'm not making it up," Jill said.

"Honest, it was in a book."

"It's more likely a two-legged fox," Alice's mother said. "You be careful."

"I can't see Fay Cow standing there while a fox nibbles at her," Alice said. "Still, the mystery will be solved tomorrow."

"Won't it be a bit boring?" Jill said.

"Great detectives are *never* bored," Alice said.

Chapter 3

But they were.

Jill thought that just in case it was a two-legged fox, they'd better hide in the wood and watch Fay Cow from there. And so, after breakfast, they took their packets of elevenses-picnic and settled themselves under the trees, over the wall from where Fay Cow was sitting.

It wasn't a big success.

First of all, Fay Cow moved off and sat somewhere else, so that they couldn't see her; and then she

got up and stood around for a long
time doing nothing. Alice and Jill
ate their buns and strawberry-jam
sandwiches, and played bears and
Hansel and Gretel, and suddenly
realised that Fay Cow had
disappeared. There was nothing in
the field except two birds, which got
up and flew away over the lane.

Alice and Jill looked at each other. First disappearing milk, now a disappearing cow.

"Listen," Alice said. Across the far side of the field from Fay Cow's barn, there was the faint clanking of buckets. Alice and Jill very carefully climbed out of the wood, and crept around the edge of the field to Fay Cow's yard. The gate was open and there was the sound of milking in the barn. Neither of them felt very brave, and so they very quietly climbed the stone wall, and sat under the twisted plum trees where the two-legged fox wouldn't see them when it came out of the barn.

After a few minutes, there was more banging of buckets, and Fay Cow came out of the doorway, and then Simon's mother. She was singing. She closed the gate and went away over the field without seeing them.

"She looks very happy," Jill said. She thought that it was a happy thing to be doing, anyway, milking.

A voice behind them said, "That's because my dad's coming home for good tomorrow."

Alice and Jill turned round very quickly and backed against the wall. Simon was sitting on a branch of the old plum tree behind them. Jill clenched her fist.

Simon said, "It's the first time she's been happy for ages." He climbed down. "Look, I'm sorry I pushed you. Sorry I've been so horrible."

Alice thought about her elbow, and then about the deal with her mother, and said, "We won't be horrible if you aren't." Her voice wasn't exactly friendly. She looked round and saw Jill looking at her. She seemed to have forgotten being pushed off the churchyard wall.

Alice said, "Oh, all right. Be friends. Would you like to come down to my house? It'll just be time for elevenses."

"Again?" Jill said.

"Why not?" Alice said. "It's always time for elevenses at our house. And we've got lots of strawberries."

They went down through the woods and across the stream, and when they got to Alice's house there were three dishes of strawberries and Fayicecream waiting on the

doorstep, and Alice's mother was being very noisy in the cellar.

They played on the slide (without pushing) and then they played damming the stream, and then they took turns to cheddar the curd, and the day was nice.

After Simon and Jill had gone home, and Alice was undamming the stream again, Alice's mother said, "Did you see any foxes?"

"No," Alice said. "Simon's mummy was doing the milking."

"At eleven o'clock?"

"About that, I suppose," Alice said.

"Oh," her mother said. "So that's it."

Chapter 4

That evening, Alice and Jill were standing on the second bar of the five-bar gate, watching Alice's mother trying to persuade Fay Cow to come in for the supper-time milking. It was really Simon's mother's turn, but she was getting ready for Simon's father to come home, and she and Simon were very busy and cheerful.

It had been a nice, long, hot, smelly afternoon. They had helped to clean out Fay Cow's barn, carrying forkfuls of muck across to

the huge compost heap. Then
they'd washed under the tap beside
the barn, and had more jam
sandwiches. Now Fay Cow had
found a delicious piece of grass, and
was not thinking of moving too
quickly.

"Simon's not bad, is he?" Jill said. "Really."

Alice looked at the scrape on her elbow. "I suppose he isn't," she said, at last.

"I wonder why his daddy went away?" Jill said.

"Grown-ups do that sort of thing, don't they," Alice said. "But it looks as if it's all right now."

"Friends," Jill said.

Fay Cow got up, after some prodding, and ambled towards them. Behind her, the sky was turning gold.

"I wonder if there'll be less milk tonight," Jill said. They climbed off the gate and dragged it back over the dried mud. "I mean, somebody could have sneaked some milk when we weren't looking. Or it really could be foxes."

"Don't be silly," Alice said. "Of course there'll be less milk. And it isn't foxes."

"How do you know?"

"There'll be less milk because Fay Cow's had less time to fill up since this morning. She usually gets milked at seven o'clock; this morning, Simon's mummy didn't milk her until eleven."

"You mean, all those times when there was less milk, it was because Simon's mummy got up late."

"And she got up late because she was tired."

"And now Simon's daddy's coming home, she won't be."

"Ah," Jill said.

Fay Cow rolled past them into the yard. Alice leaned forward and patted her on the nose.

"Lots of cream tonight, please, Fay Cow. Simon's daddy'll need some on his strawberries."